Mr. Kazarian
Alien Librarian

by Steve Foxe
illustrated by Gary Boller

STONE ARCH BOOKS
a capstone imprint

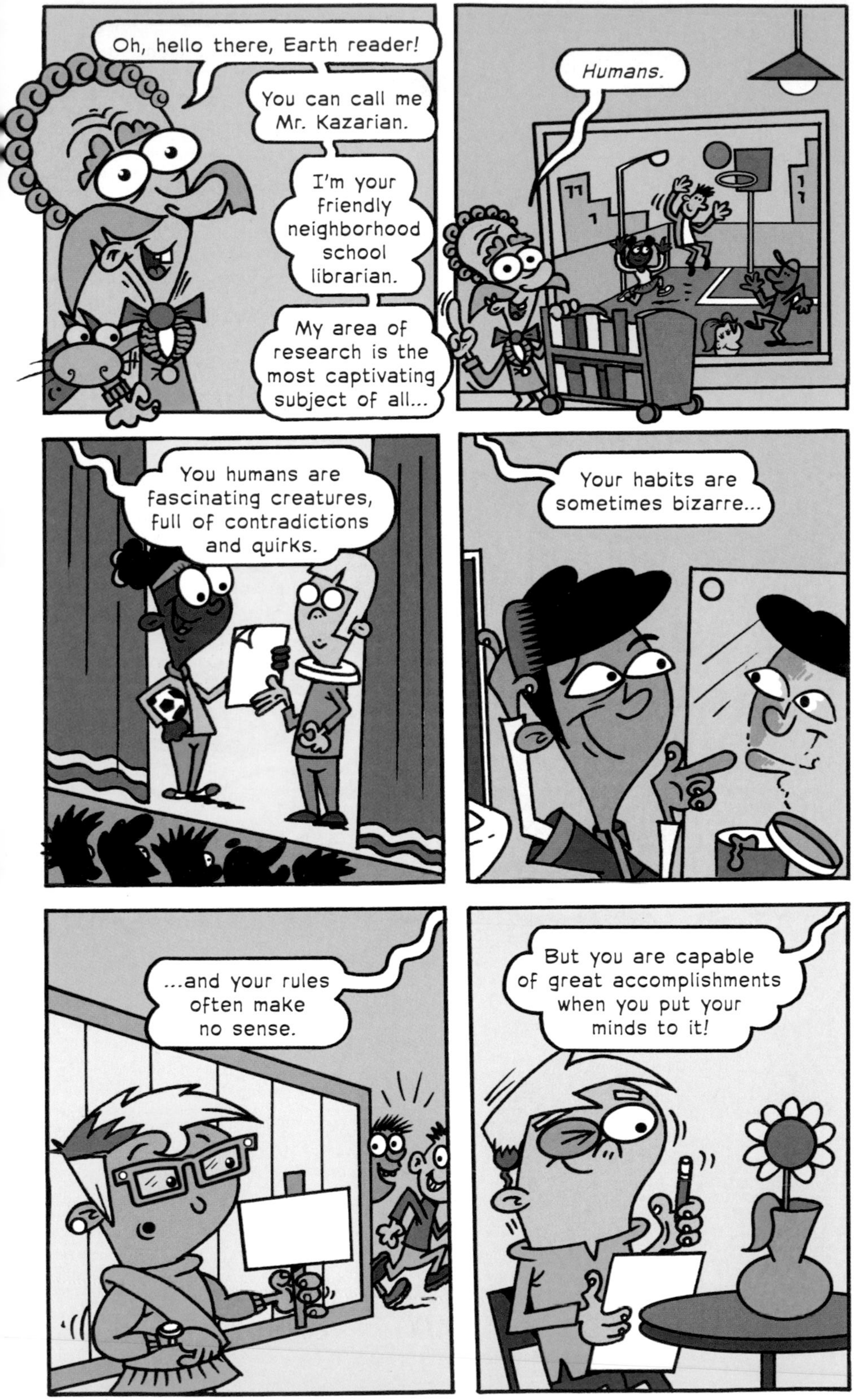

Oh, hello there, Earth reader!
You can call me Mr. Kazarian.
I'm your friendly neighborhood school librarian.
My area of research is the most captivating subject of all...
Humans.
You humans are fascinating creatures, full of contradictions and quirks.
Your habits are sometimes bizarre...
...and your rules often make no sense.
But you are capable of great accomplishments when you put your minds to it!

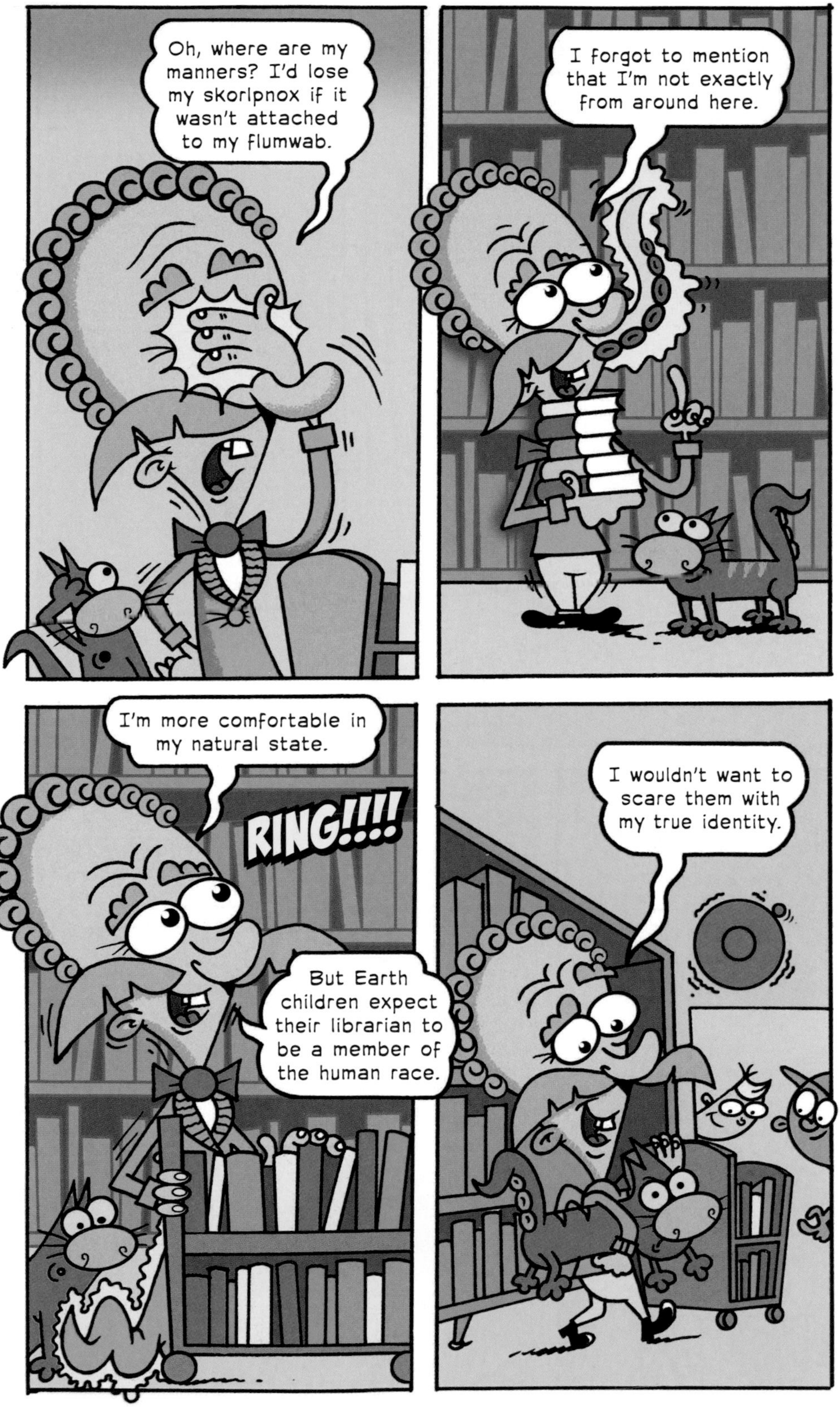
Oh, where are my manners? I'd lose my skorlpnox if it wasn't attached to my flumwab.
I forgot to mention that I'm not exactly from around here.
I'm more comfortable in my natural state.
RING!!!!
But Earth children expect their librarian to be a member of the human race.
I wouldn't want to scare them with my true identity.

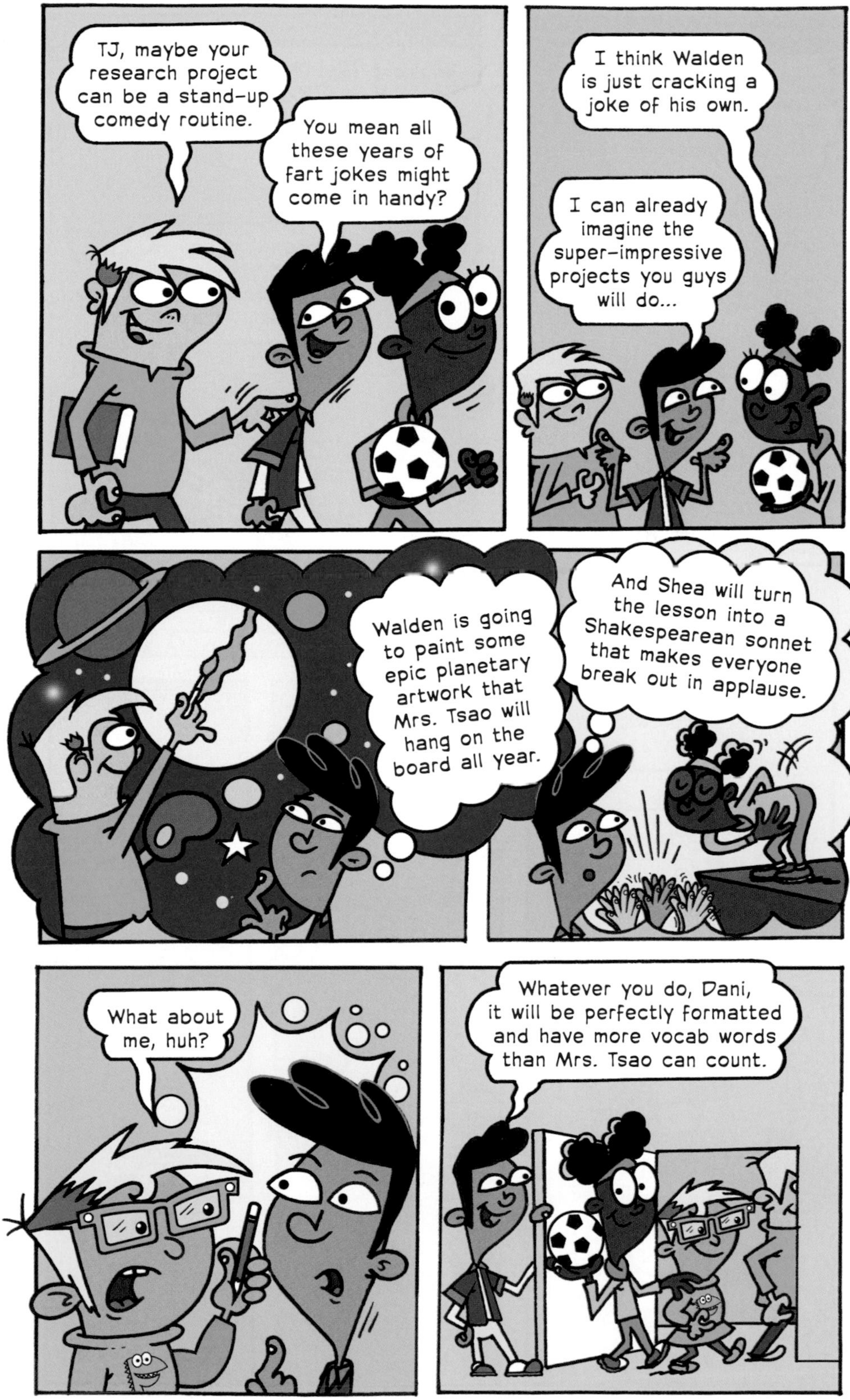
TJ, maybe your research project can be a stand-up comedy routine.
You mean all these years of fart jokes might come in handy?
I think Walden is just cracking a joke of his own.
I can already imagine the super-impressive projects you guys will do...
Walden is going to paint some epic planetary artwork that Mrs. Tsao will hang on the board all year.
And Shea will turn the lesson into a Shakespearean sonnet that makes everyone break out in applause.
What about me, huh?
Whatever you do, Dani, it will be perfectly formatted and have more vocab words than Mrs. Tsao can count.

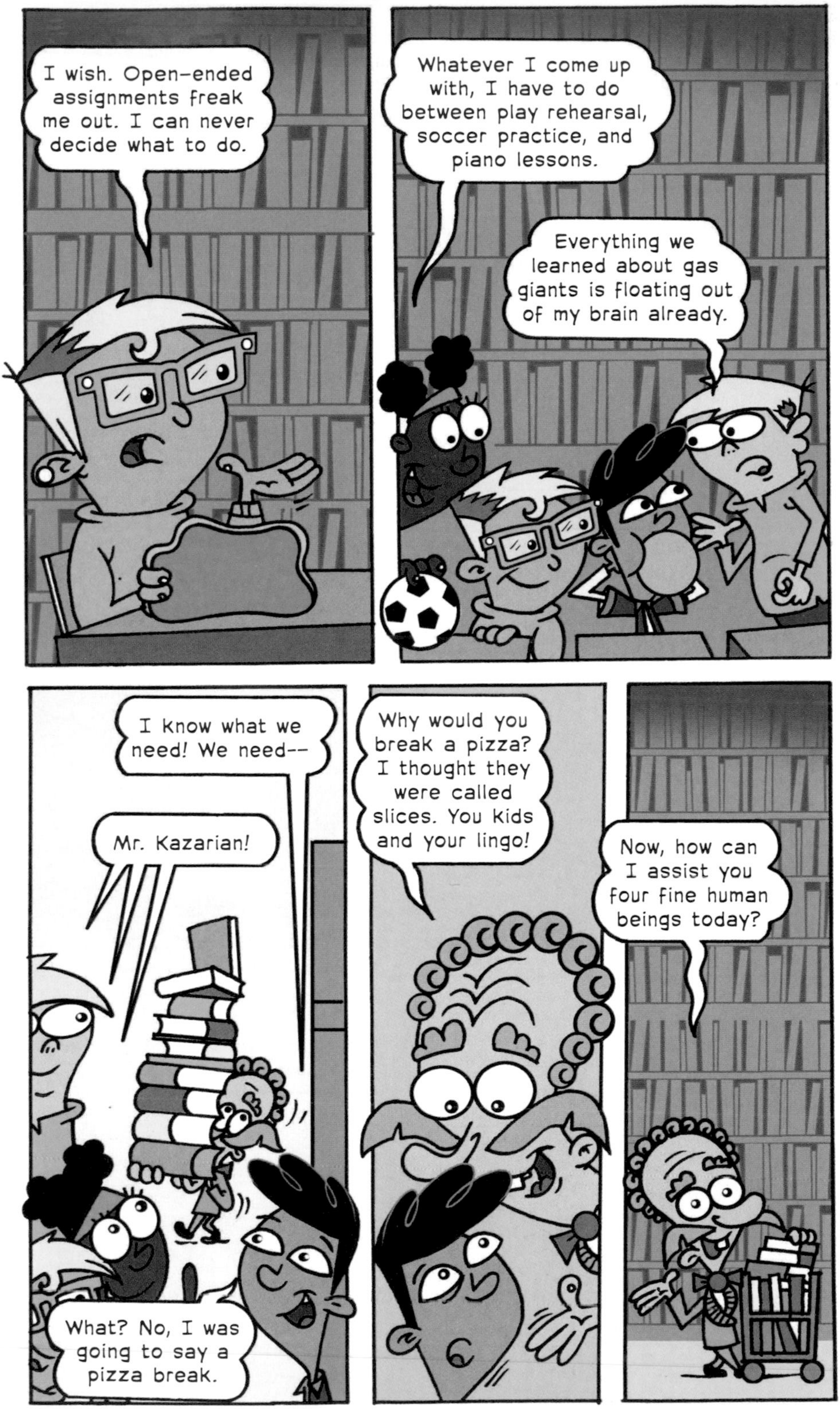
I wish. Open-ended assignments freak me out. I can never decide what to do.
Whatever I come up with, I have to do between play rehearsal, soccer practice, and piano lessons.
Everything we learned about gas giants is floating out of my brain already.
I know what we need! We need--
Mr. Kazarian!
What? No, I was going to say a pizza break.
Why would you break a pizza? I thought they were called slices. You kids and your lingo!
Now, how can I assist you four fine human beings today?

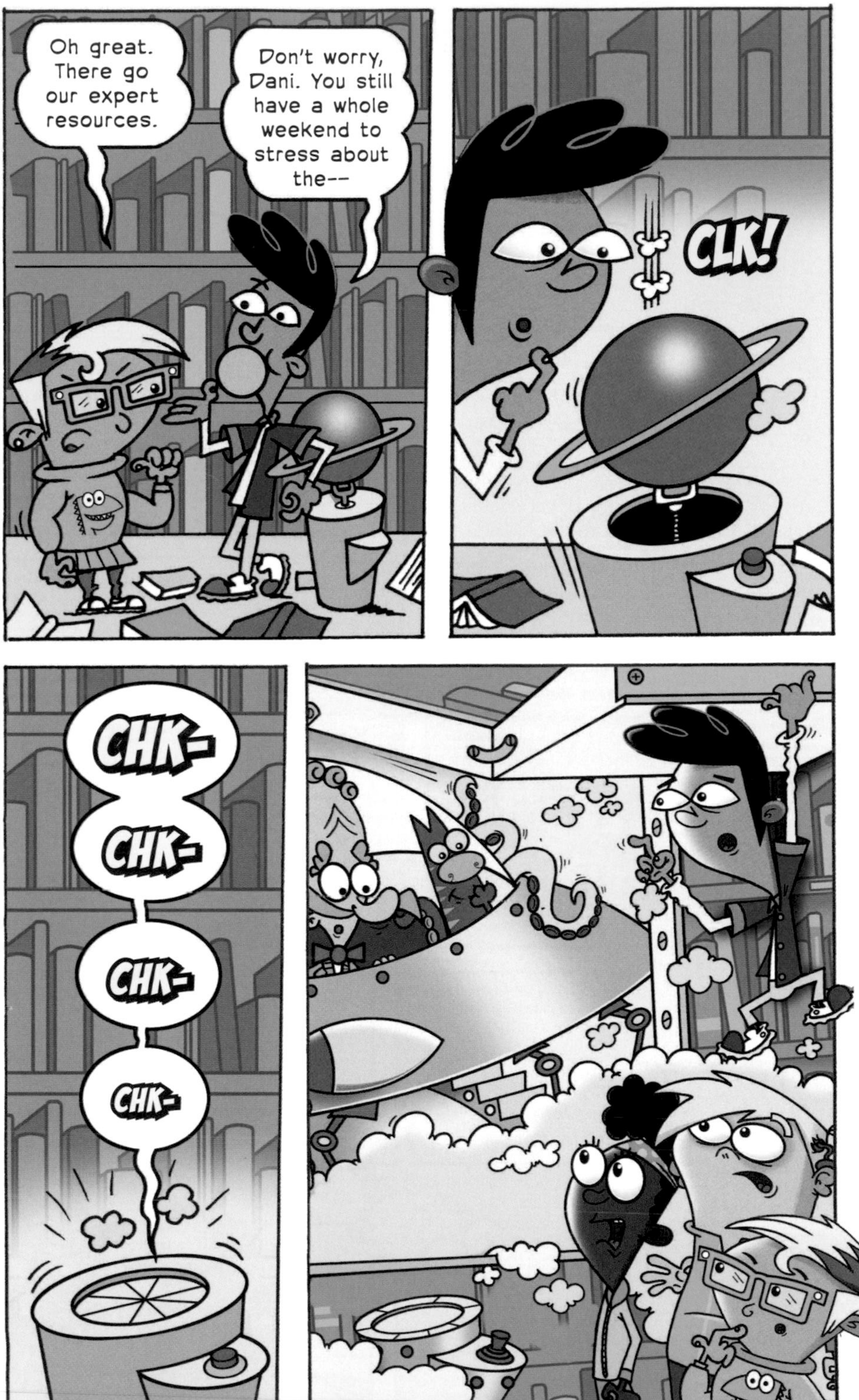
Oh great. There go our expert resources.
Don't worry, Dani. You still have a whole weekend to stress about the--
CLK!
CHK-
CHK-
CHK-
CHK-

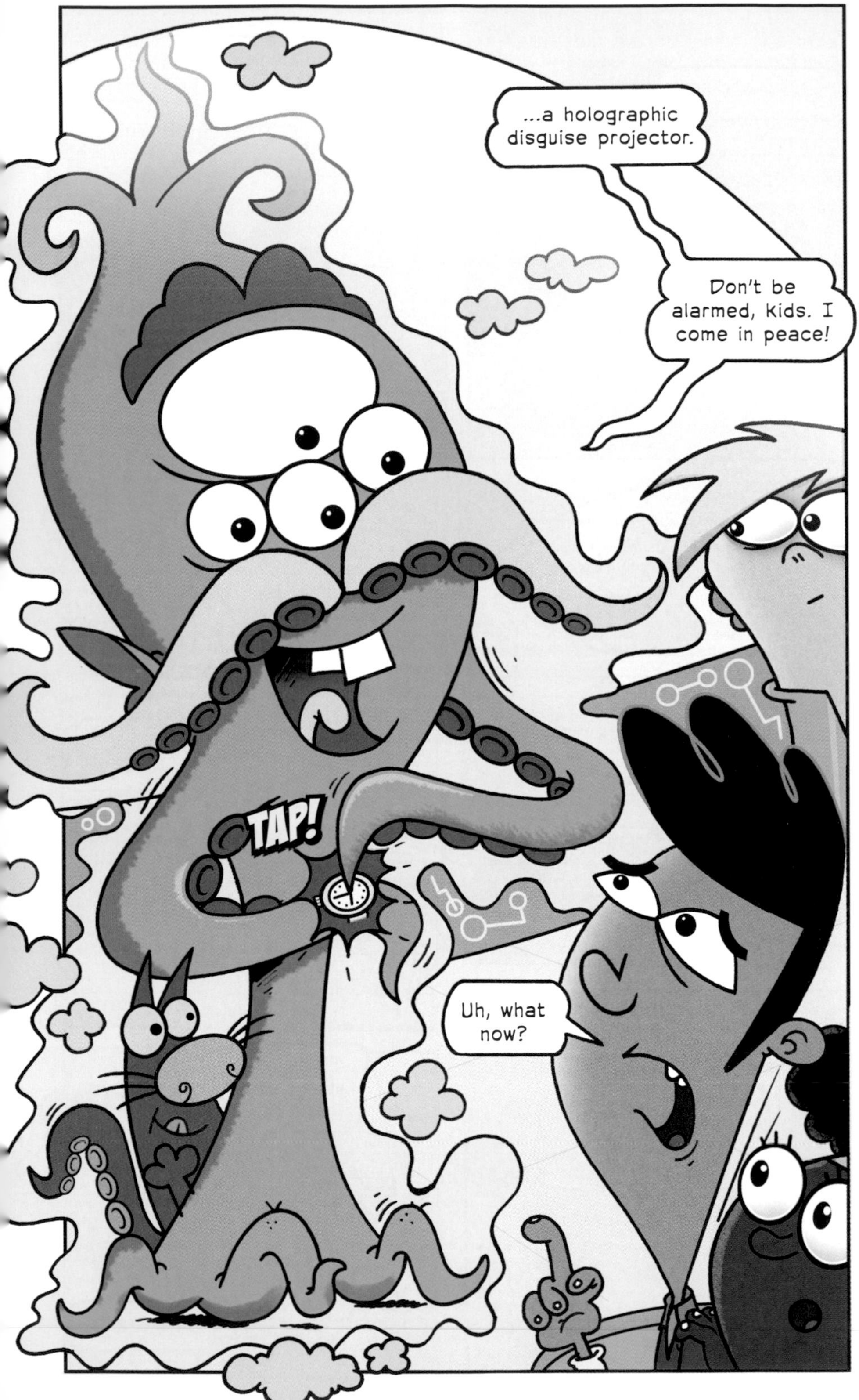
...a holographic disguise projector.
Don't be alarmed, kids. I come in peace!
TAP!
Uh, what now?

11

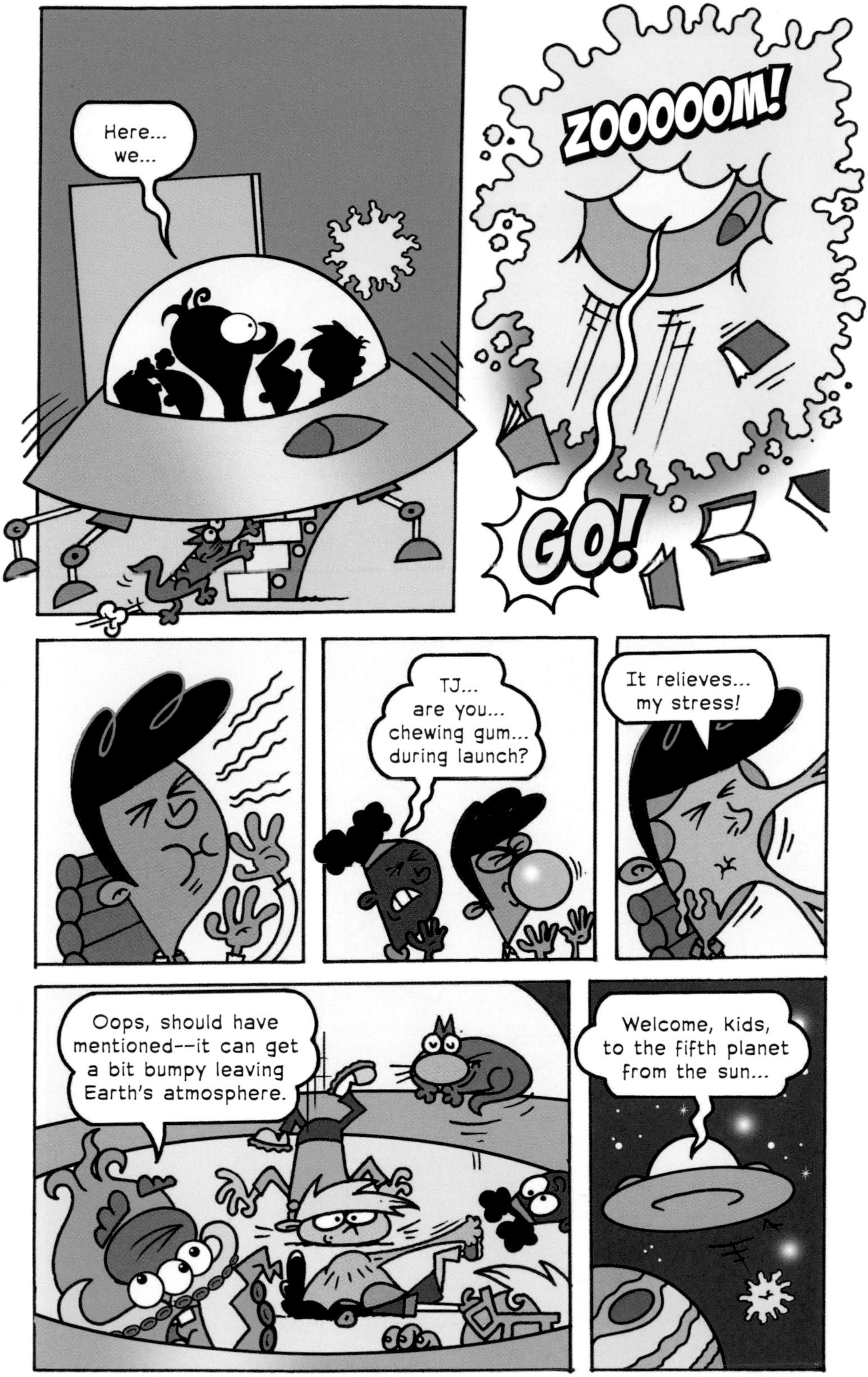
Here... we...
ZOOOOOM!
GO!
TJ... are you... chewing gum... during launch?
It relieves... my stress!
Oops, should have mentioned--it can get a bit bumpy leaving Earth's atmosphere.
Welcome, kids, to the fifth planet from the sun...

14

18

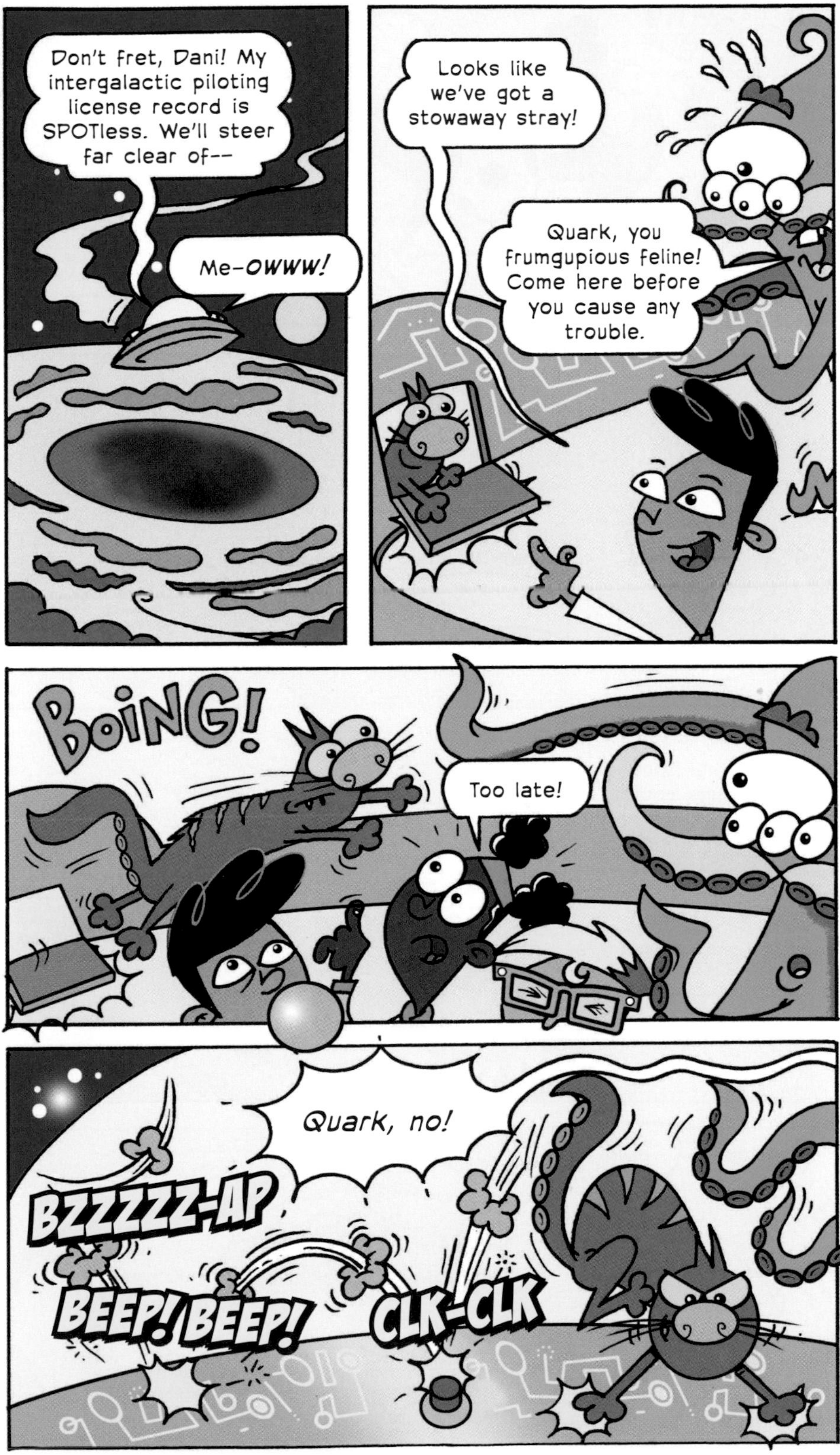

Don't fret, Dani! My intergalactic piloting license record is SPOTless. We'll steer far clear of--
Me-OWWW!
Looks like we've got a stowaway stray!
Quark, you frumgupious feline! Come here before you cause any trouble.
BOiNG!
Too late!
Quark, no!
BZZZZZ-AP
BEEP! BEEP!
CLK-CLK

24

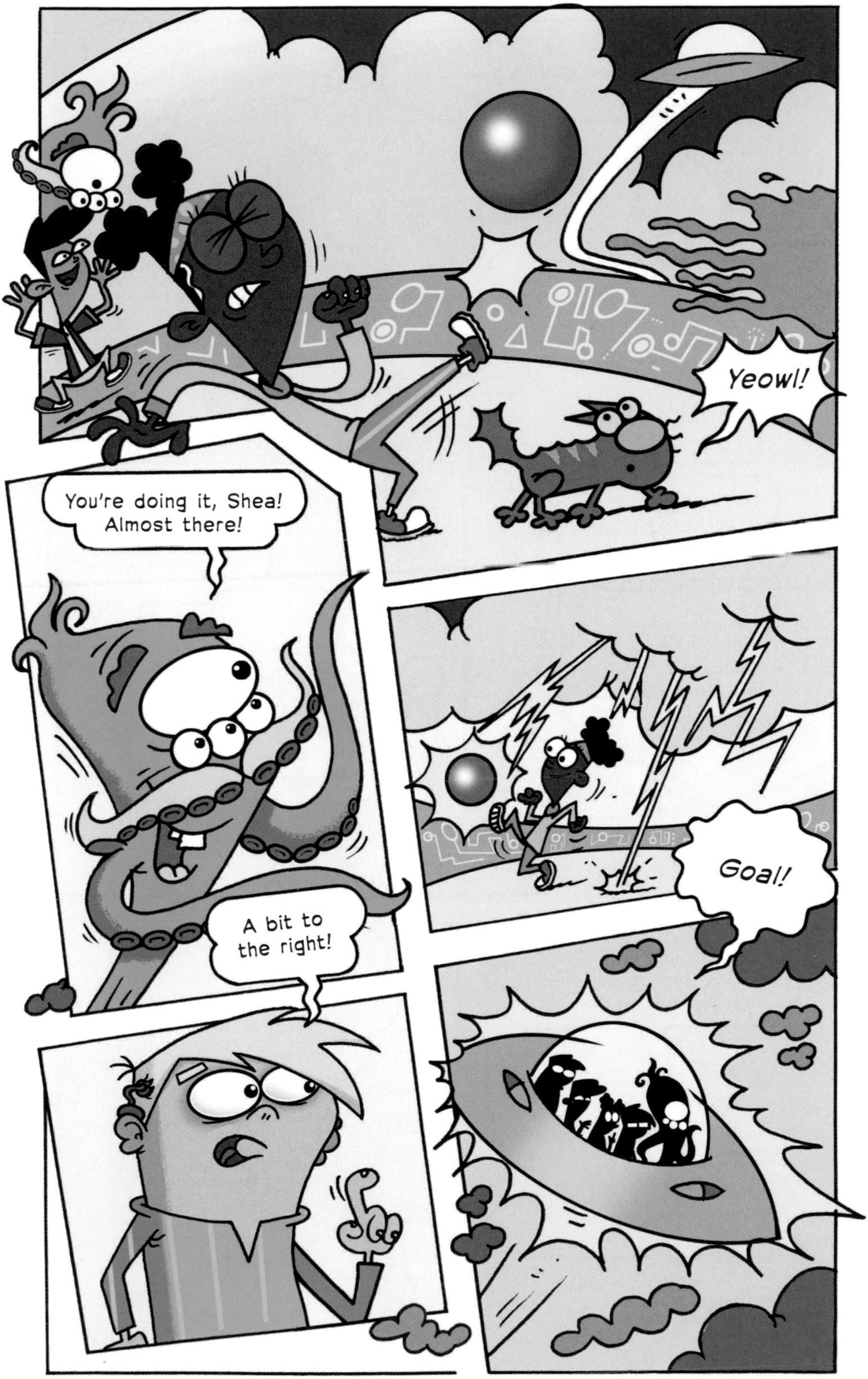
Yeowl!
You're doing it, Shea! Almost there!
A bit to the right!
Goal!

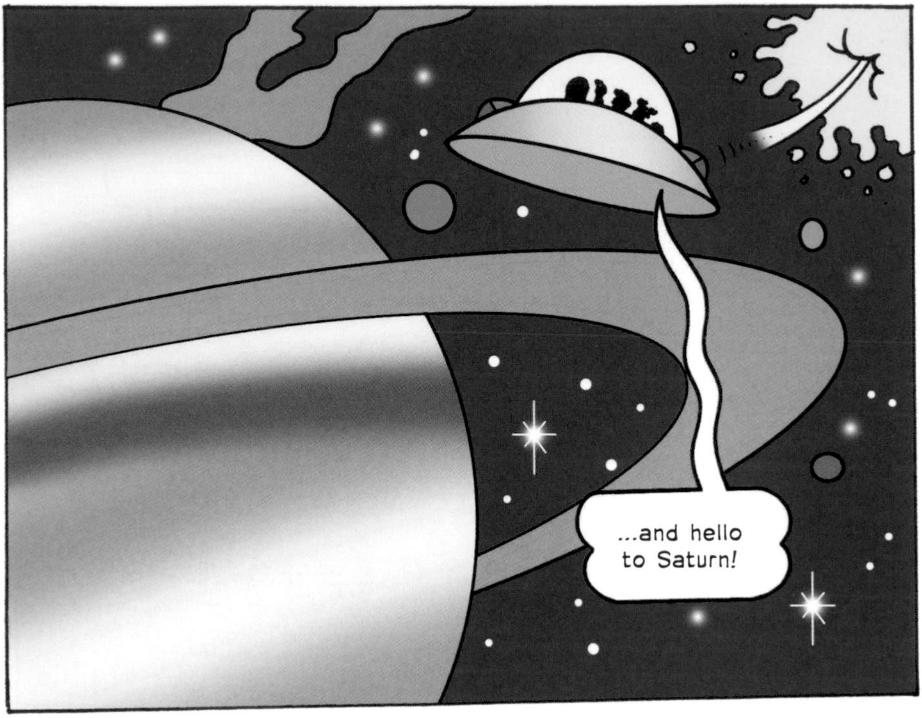
...and hello to Saturn!

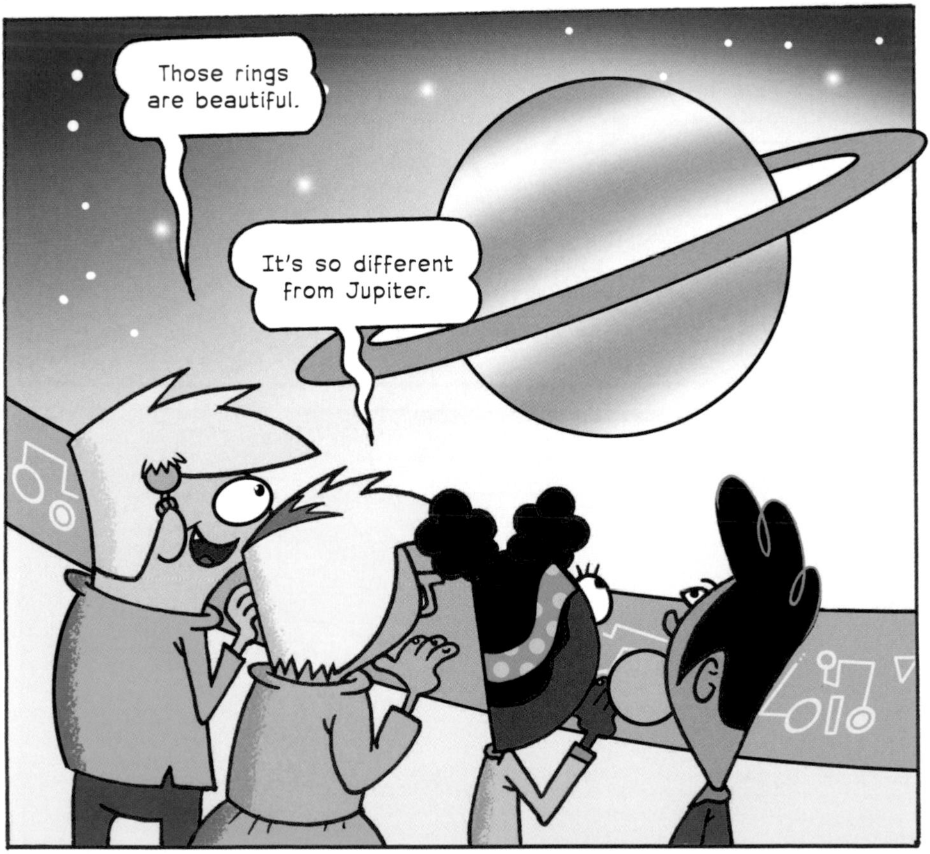
Those rings are beautiful.
It's so different from Jupiter.

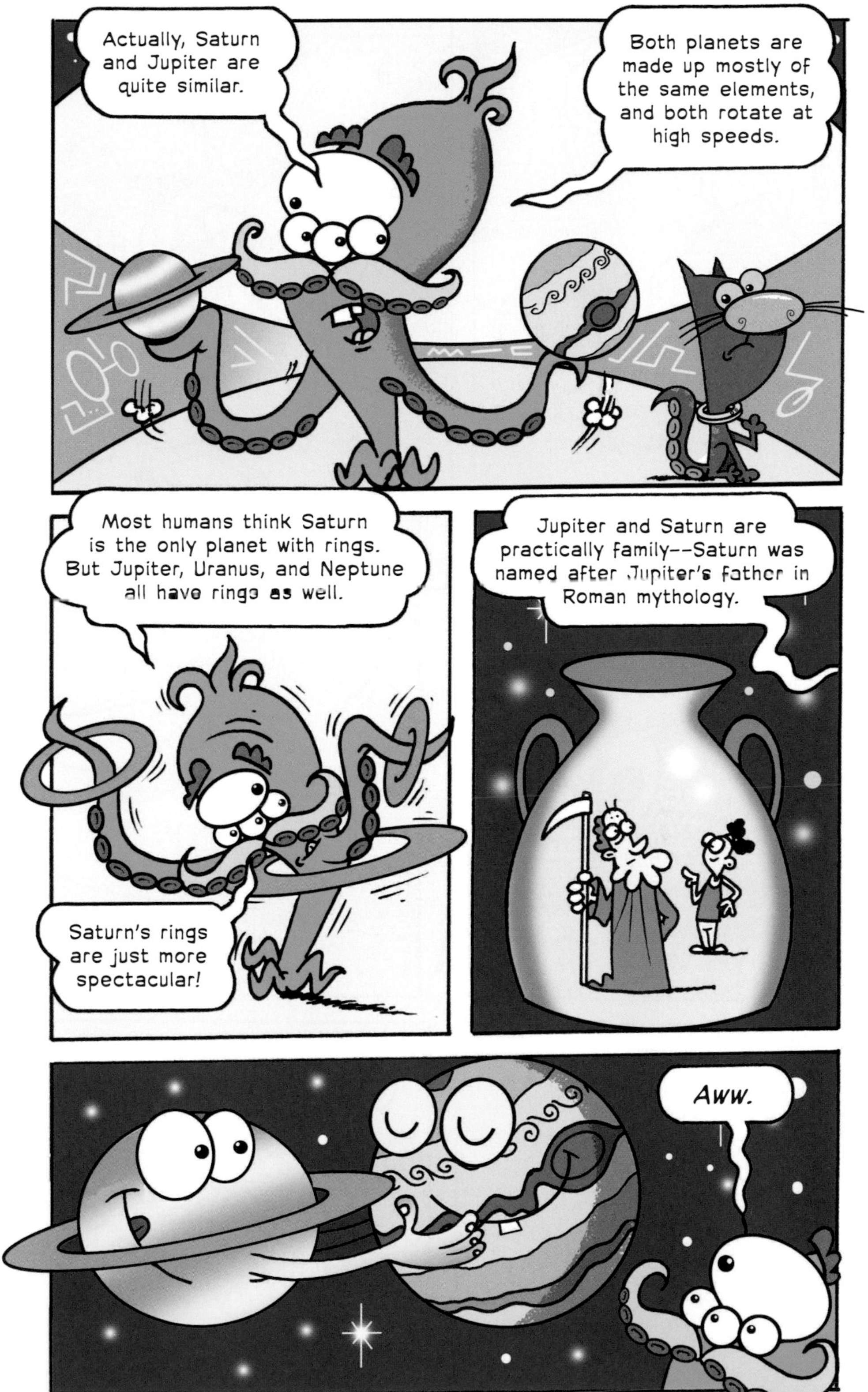

Actually, Saturn and Jupiter are quite similar.
Both planets are made up mostly of the same elements, and both rotate at high speeds.
Most humans think Saturn is the only planet with rings. But Jupiter, Uranus, and Neptune all have rings as well.
Saturn's rings are just more spectacular!
Jupiter and Saturn are practically family--Saturn was named after Jupiter's father in Roman mythology.
Aww.

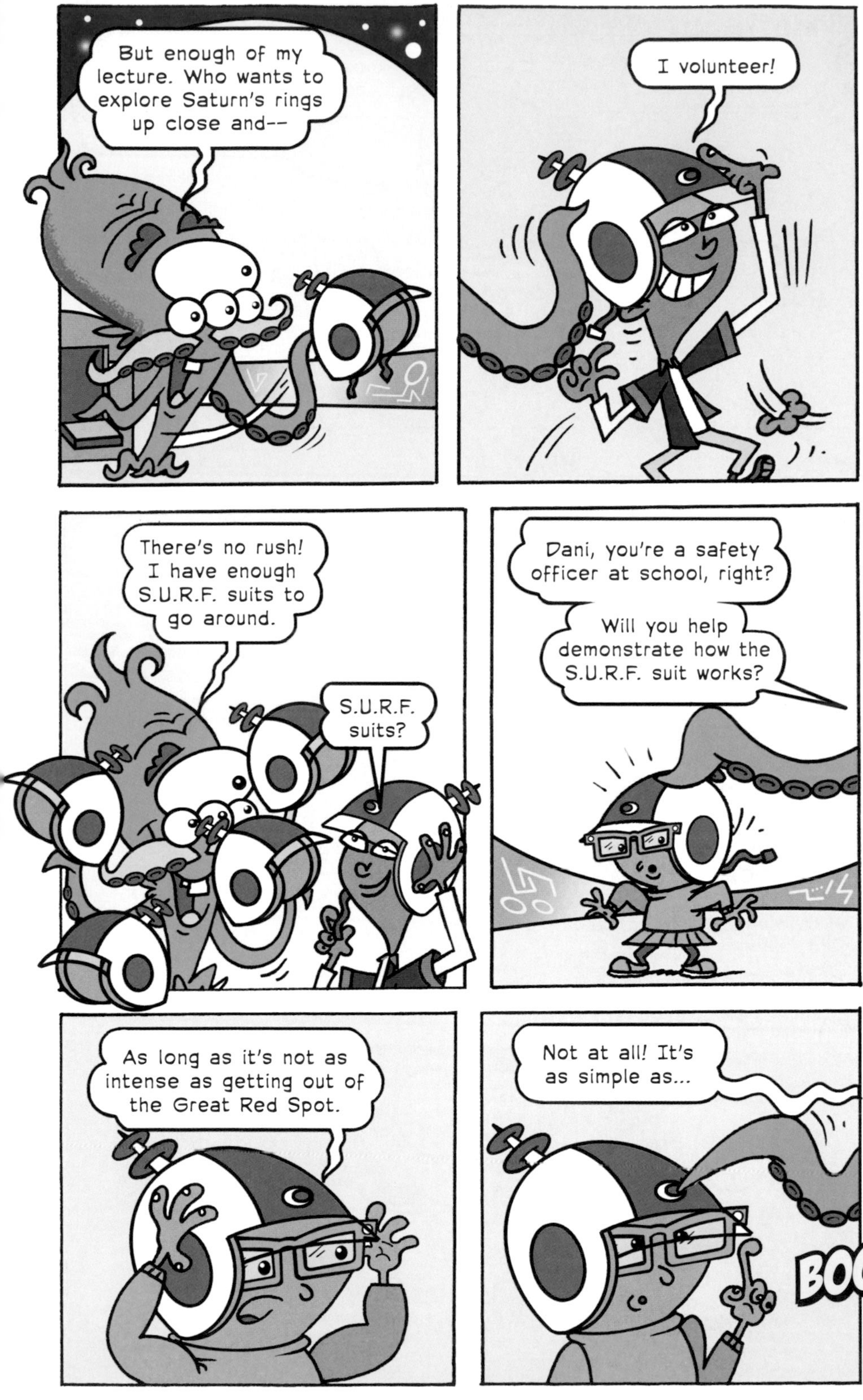
But enough of my lecture. Who wants to explore Saturn's rings up close and--
I volunteer!
There's no rush! I have enough S.U.R.F. suits to go around.
S.U.R.F. suits?
Dani, you're a safety officer at school, right?
Will you help demonstrate how the S.U.R.F. suit works?
As long as it's not as intense as getting out of the Great Red Spot.
Not at all! It's as simple as...
BOOP!

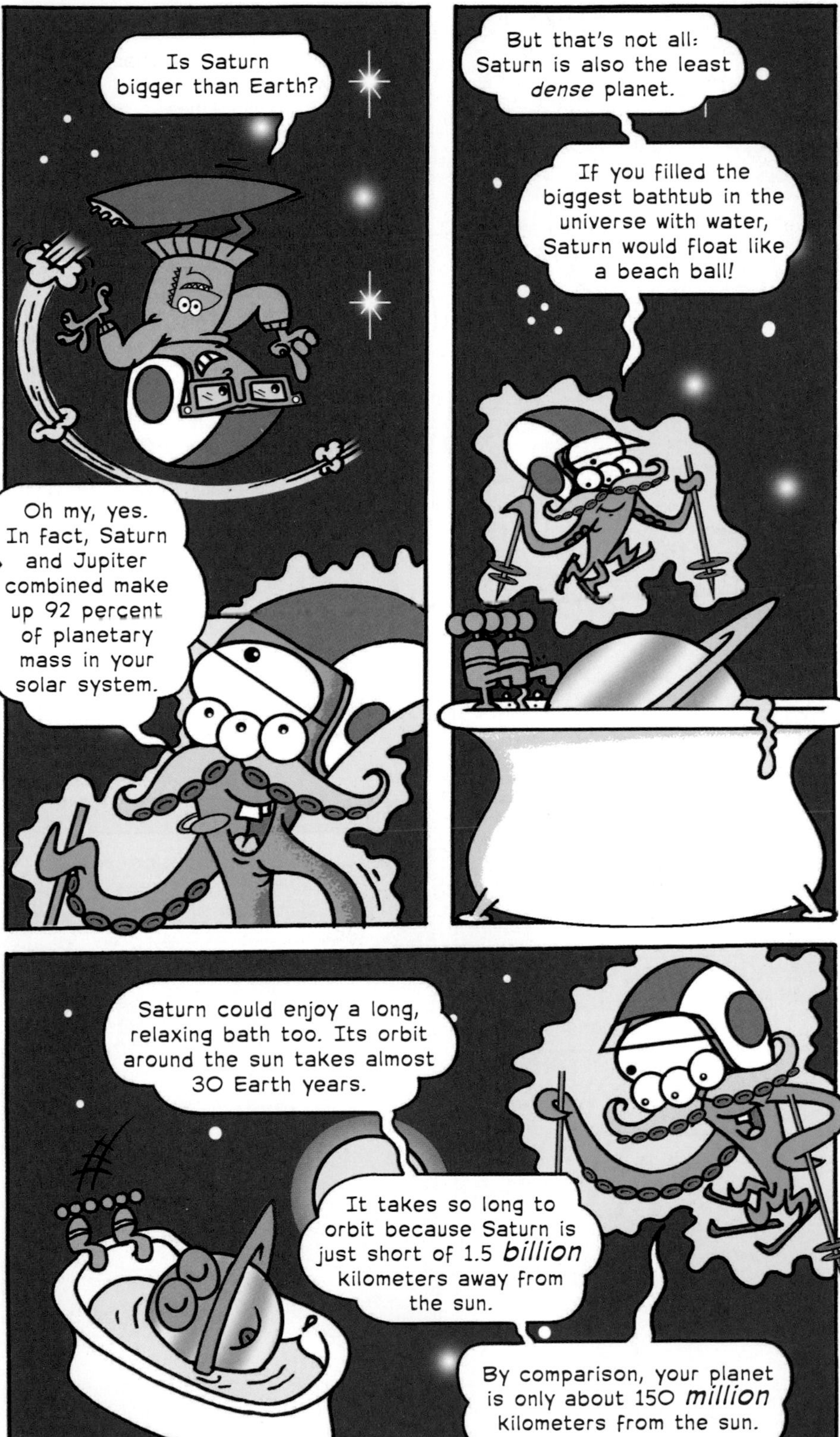
Is Saturn bigger than Earth?
Oh my, yes. In fact, Saturn and Jupiter combined make up 92 percent of planetary mass in your solar system.
But that's not all: Saturn is also the least *dense* planet.
If you filled the biggest bathtub in the universe with water, Saturn would float like a beach ball!
Saturn could enjoy a long, relaxing bath too. Its orbit around the sun takes almost 30 Earth years.
It takes so long to orbit because Saturn is just short of 1.5 *billion* kilometers away from the sun.
By comparison, your planet is only about 150 *million* kilometers from the sun.

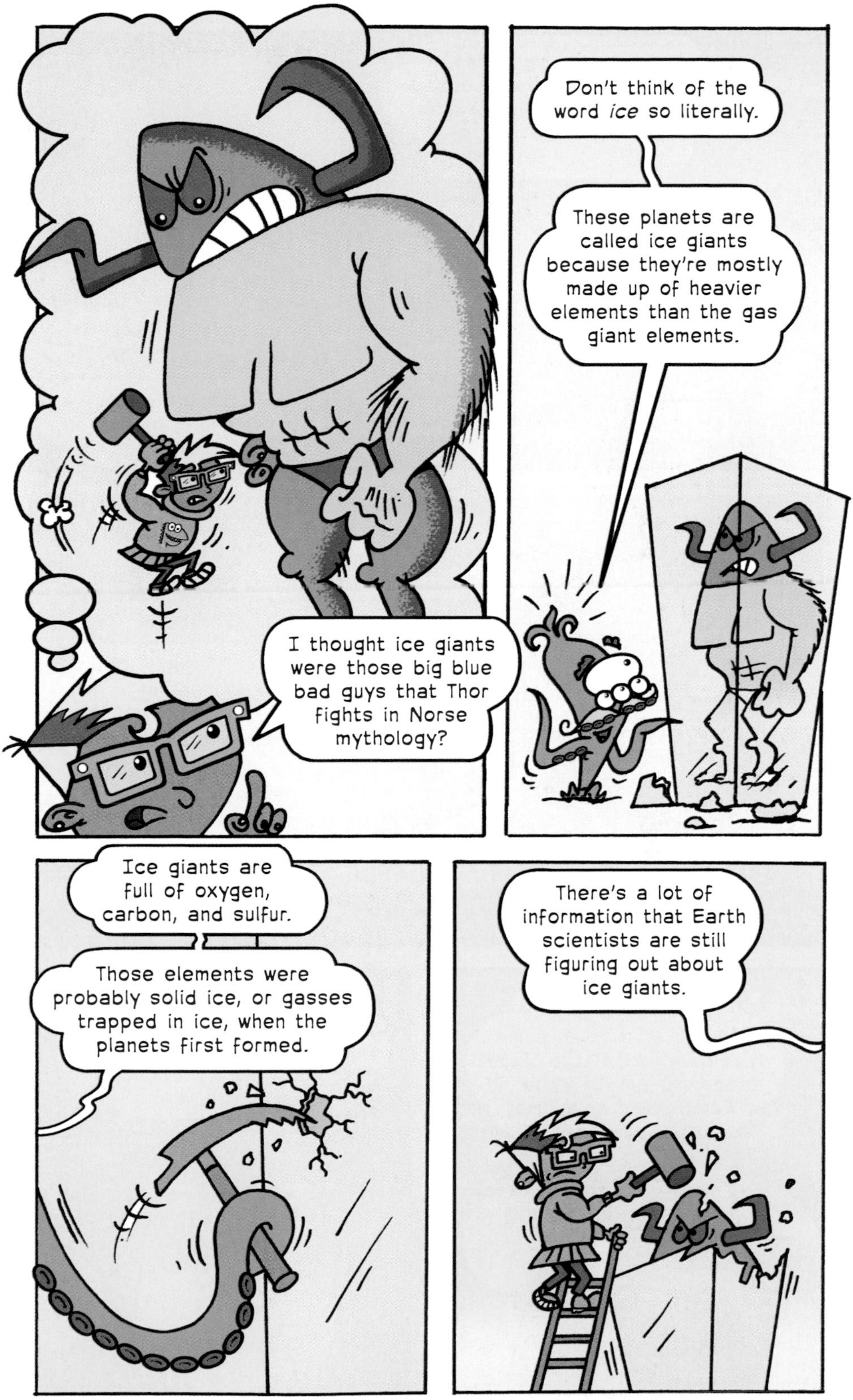
I thought ice giants were those big blue bad guys that Thor fights in Norse mythology?
Don't think of the word *ice* so literally.
These planets are called ice giants because they're mostly made up of heavier elements than the gas giant elements.
Ice giants are full of oxygen, carbon, and sulfur.
Those elements were probably solid ice, or gasses trapped in ice, when the planets first formed.
There's a lot of information that Earth scientists are still figuring out about ice giants.

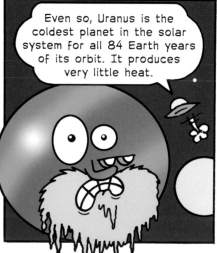

41

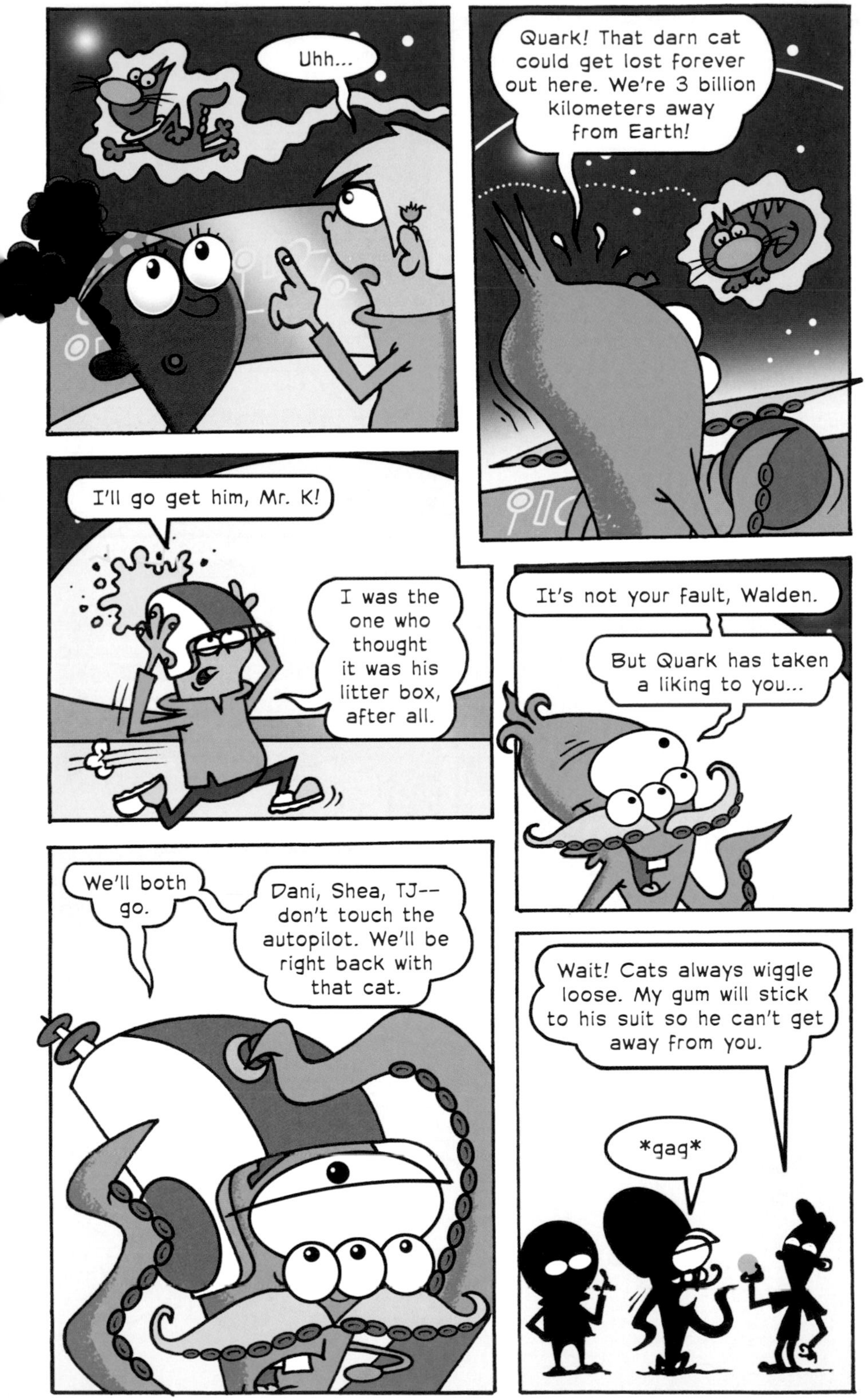
Uhh...
Quark! That darn cat could get lost forever out here. We're 3 billion kilometers away from Earth!
I'll go get him, Mr. K!
I was the one who thought it was his litter box, after all.
It's not your fault, Walden.
But Quark has taken a liking to you...
We'll both go.
Dani, Shea, TJ-- don't touch the autopilot. We'll be right back with that cat.
Wait! Cats always wiggle loose. My gum will stick to his suit so he can't get away from you.
gag

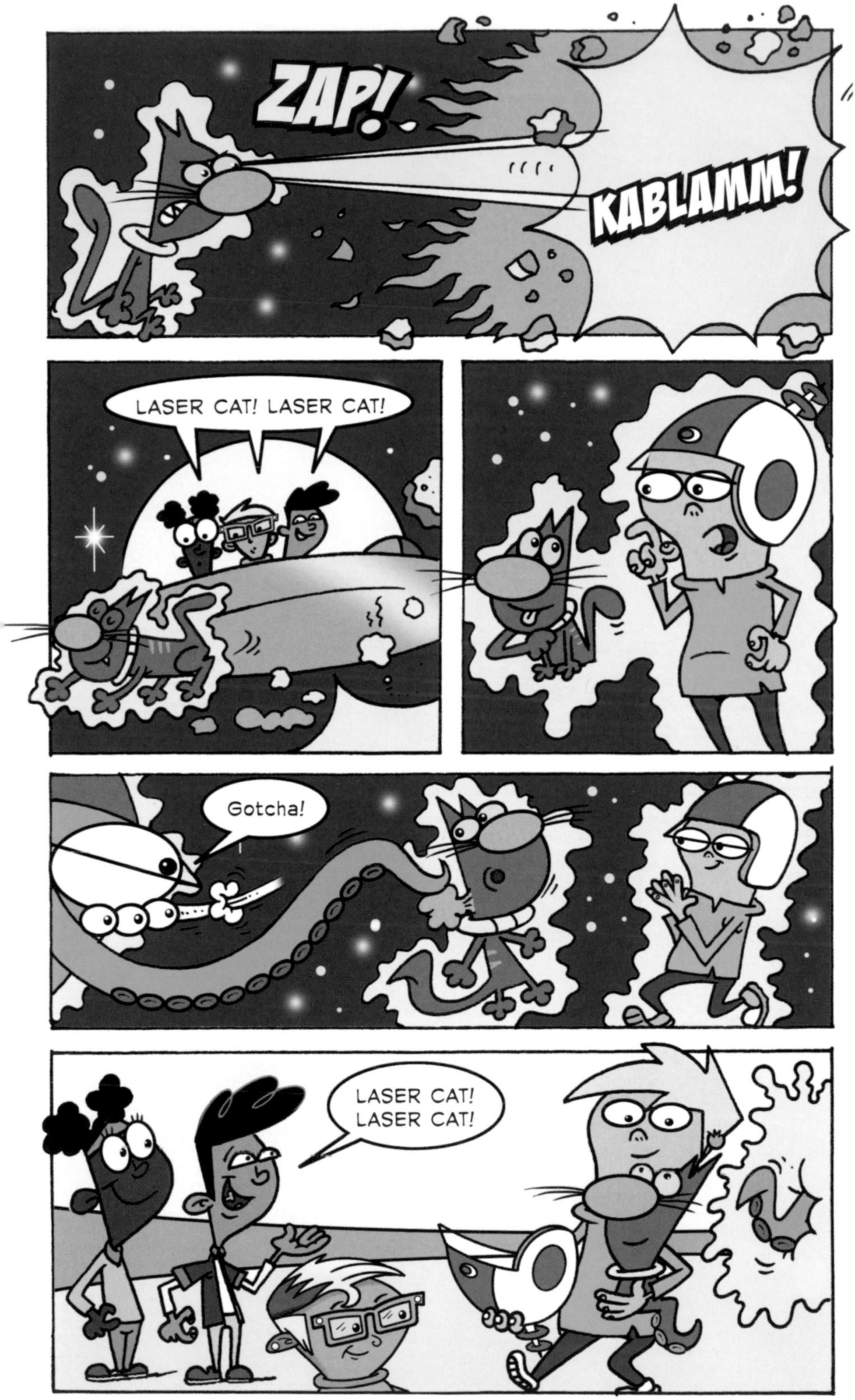
ZAP!
KABLAMM!
LASER CAT! LASER CAT!
Gotcha!
LASER CAT! LASER CAT!

45

Neptune has an average distance from the sun of 4.5 billion kilometers.

In fact, Neptune has only completed ONE orbit since its discovery. It takes 165 Earth years to make the full journey.

Weee!

Pluto's orbit crosses with Neptune's every 250 Earth years or so. During that time Pluto is actually closer to the sun than Neptune.

PLUTO

But Pluto isn't even a planet anymore!

Correct! It was reclassified as a dwarf planet in 2006. That means Neptune is always the farthest *planet* from the sun.

Sorry, Pluto.

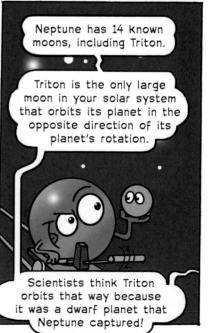

Neptune has 14 known moons, including Triton.

Triton is the only large moon in your solar system that orbits its planet in the opposite direction of its planet's rotation.

Scientists think Triton orbits that way because it was a dwarf planet that Neptune captured!

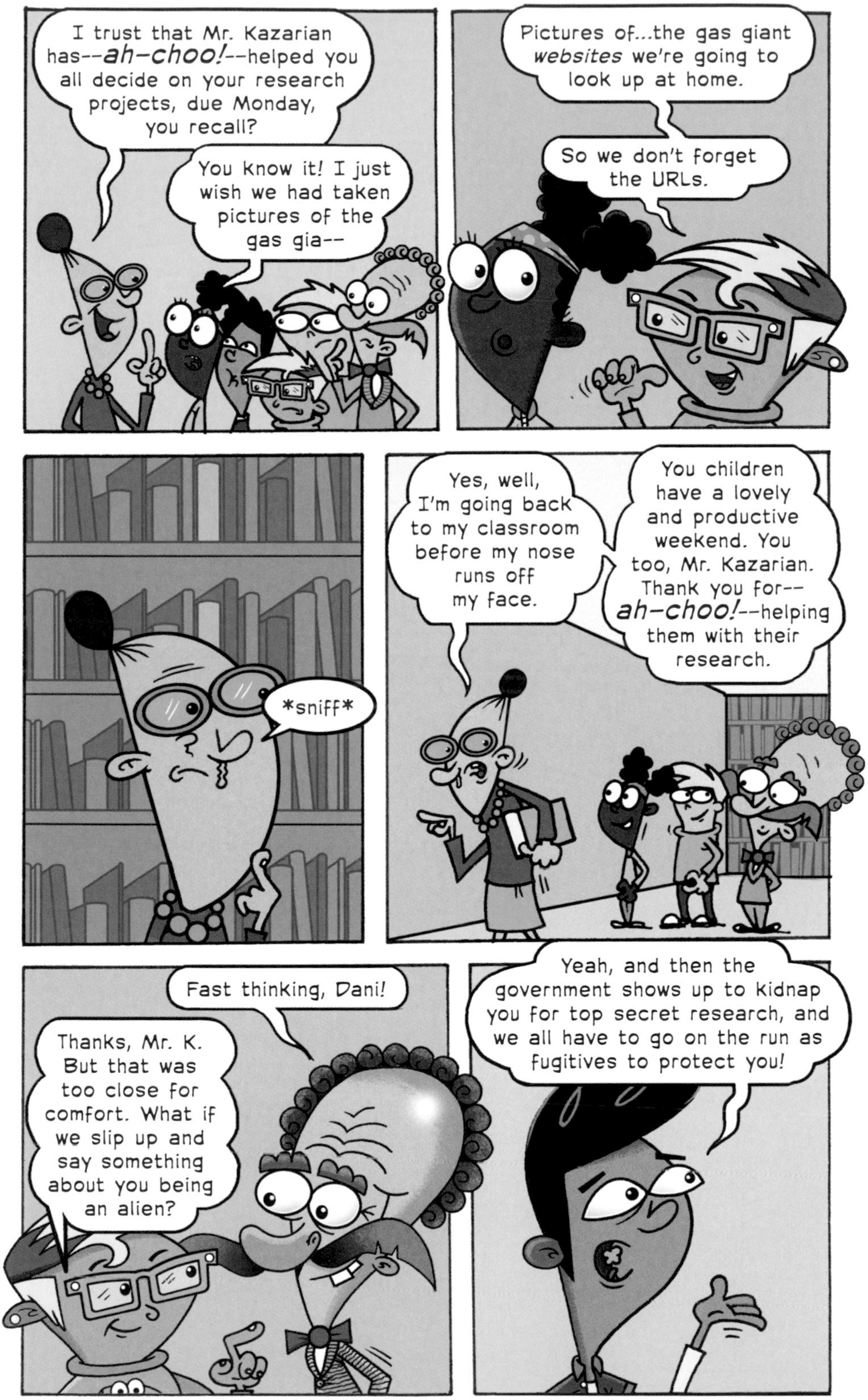
I trust that Mr. Kazarian has--*ah-choo!*--helped you all decide on your research projects, due Monday, you recall?
You know it! I just wish we had taken pictures of the gas gia--
Pictures of...the gas giant *websites* we're going to look up at home.
So we don't forget the URLs.
sniff
Yes, well, I'm going back to my classroom before my nose runs off my face.
You children have a lovely and productive weekend. You too, Mr. Kazarian. Thank you for--*ah-choo!*--helping them with their research.
Fast thinking, Dani!
Thanks, Mr. K. But that was too close for comfort. What if we slip up and say something about you being an alien?
Yeah, and then the government shows up to kidnap you for top secret research, and we all have to go on the run as fugitives to protect you!

51

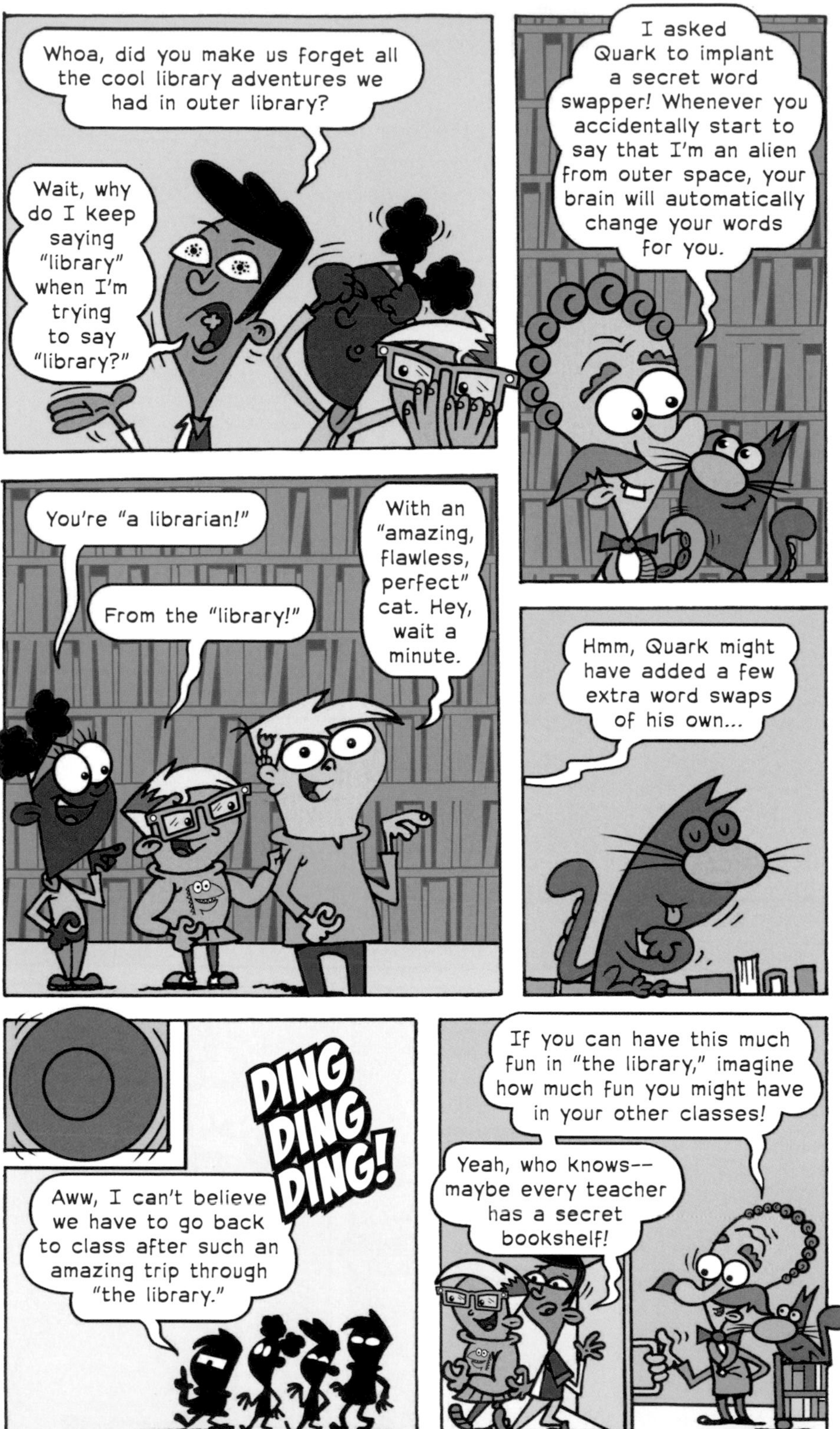
Whoa, did you make us forget all the cool library adventures we had in outer library?
Wait, why do I keep saying "library" when I'm trying to say "library?"
I asked Quark to implant a secret word swapper! Whenever you accidentally start to say that I'm an alien from outer space, your brain will automatically change your words for you.
You're "a librarian!"
From the "library!"
With an "amazing, flawless, perfect" cat. Hey, wait a minute.
Hmm, Quark might have added a few extra word swaps of his own...
DING DING DING!
Aww, I can't believe we have to go back to class after such an amazing trip through "the library."
If you can have this much fun in "the library," imagine how much fun you might have in your other classes!
Yeah, who knows-- maybe every teacher has a secret bookshelf!

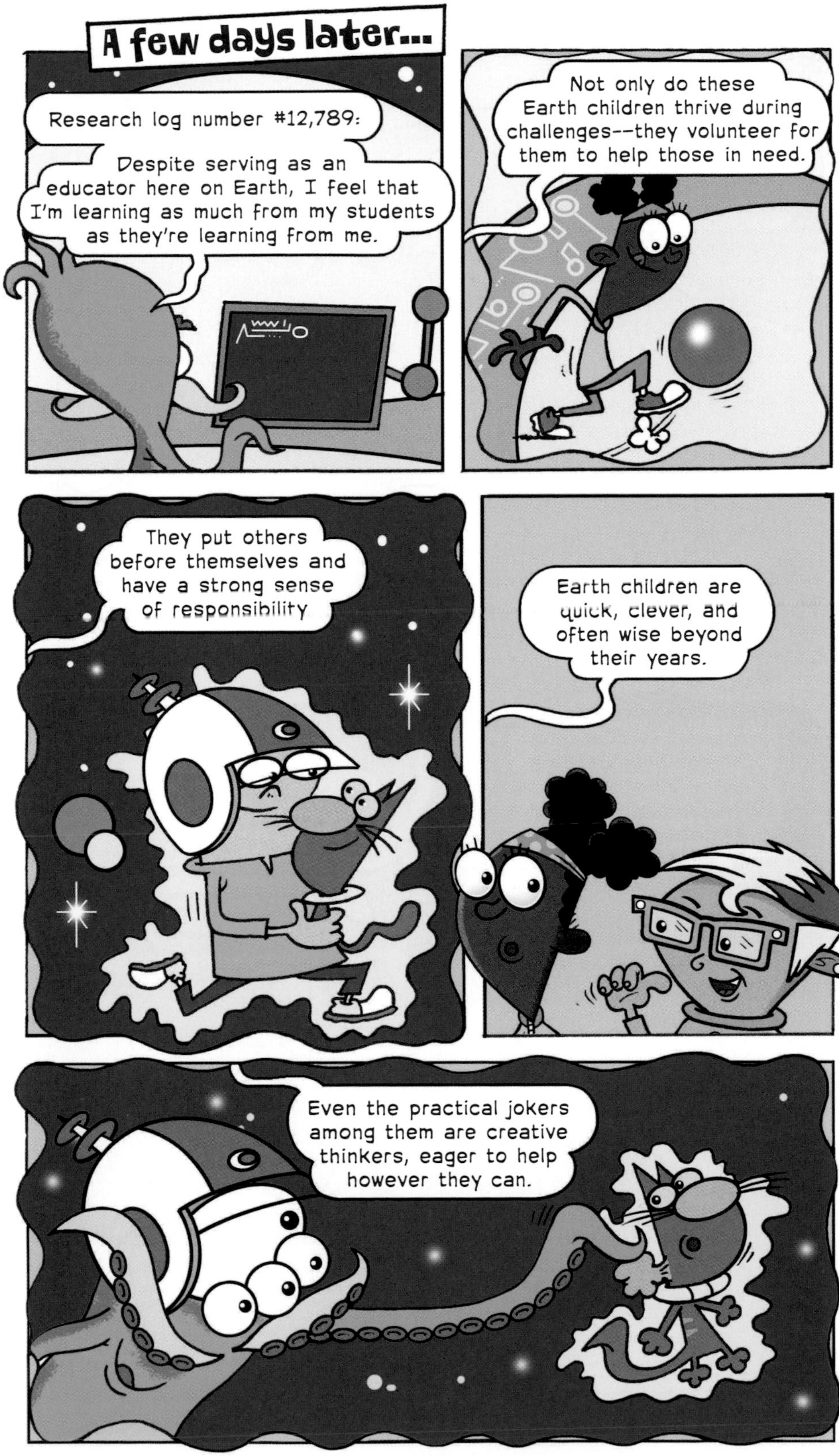
A few days later...
Research log number #12,789:
Despite serving as an educator here on Earth, I feel that I'm learning as much from my students as they're learning from me.
Not only do these Earth children thrive during challenges--they volunteer for them to help those in need.
They put others before themselves and have a strong sense of responsibility.
Earth children are quick, clever, and often wise beyond their years.
Even the practical jokers among them are creative thinkers, eager to help however they can.

57

More About
Gas Giants

These four planets were once known as Gas Giants, but Uranus and Neptune were later classified as Ice Giants.

JUPITER
5th Planet from the Sun

Composition: 90% hydrogen, 10% helium, with small amounts of ammonia, sulfur, methane, and water vapor
Diameter: 142,984 km
Mass: $1.9 \times 1,027$ kg (318 x Earth's mass)
Distance from the Sun: 778.5 million km
Orbit Period: 11.9 years

SATURN
6th Planet from the Sun

Composition: 96.3% hydrogen, 3.25% helium, with small amounts of methane and ammonia
Diameter: 115,873 km
Mass: $5.683 \times 1,026$ kg (95 x Earth's mass)
Distance from the Sun: 1.4 billion km
Orbit Period: 29.5 years

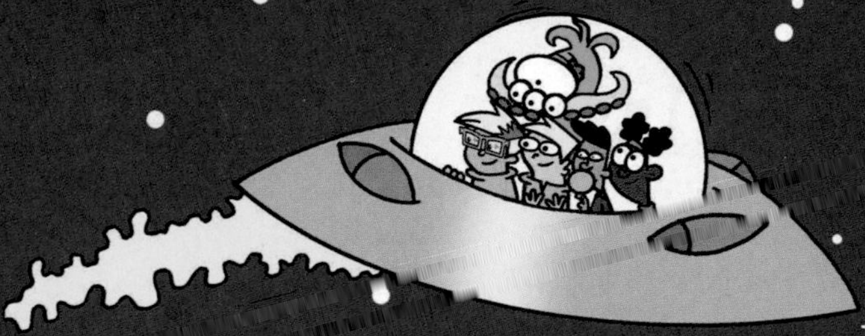

and Ice Giants

URANUS
7th Planet from the Sun

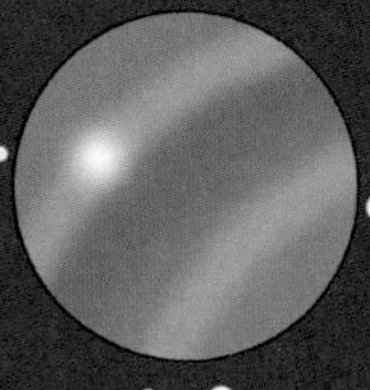

Composition: 83% hydrogen, 15% helium, and 2% methane, with a molten core
Diameter: 50,724 km
Mass: 8.681 × 1,025 kg (14.5 x Earth's mass)
Distance from the Sun: 2.8 billion km
Orbit Period: 84.0 years

NEPTUNE
8th Planet from the Sun

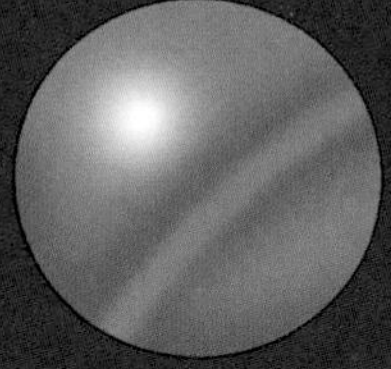

Composition: About 80% hydrogen and 19% helium, with a small amount of water and methane
Diameter: 49,244 km
Mass: 1.024 × 1,026 kg (17 x Earth's mass)
Distance from the Sun: 4.5 billion km
Orbit Period: 165 years

Glossary

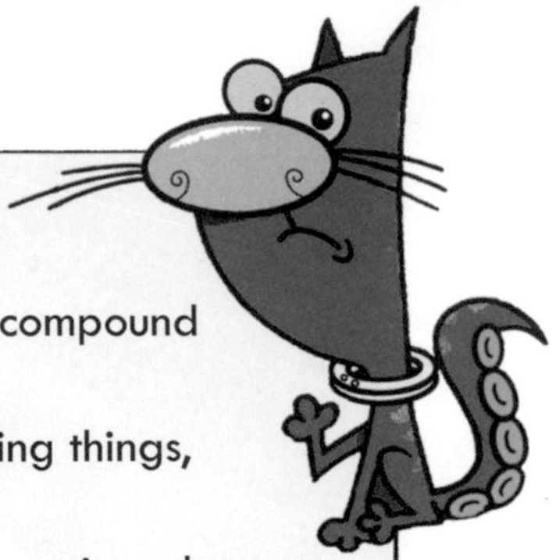

ammonia—a smelly, colorless gas that is a compound of nitrogen and hydrogen

carbon—a chemical element, found in all living things, that is the basis for life

density—the relationship of an object's mass to its volume

dwarf planet—a celestial body that orbits the sun and has a round shape but is not large enough to affect other objects in orbit

element—a substance that cannot be broken down into simpler substances

galaxy—a cluster of millions of stars bound together by gravity

gas giant—a large planet of relatively low density made mostly of hydrogen and helium; Saturn and Jupiter are gas giants

helium—a lightweight, colorless gas that does not burn

hydrogen—a colorless gas that is lighter than air and burns easily

ice giant—a large planet made mainly of substances that are heavier than helium and hydrogen; Uranus and Neptune are ice giants

kilometer—a metric unit of measurement equal to 1,000 meters, or approximately 0.62 miles

methane—a colorless, flammable gas; methane becomes a liquid at extremely cold temperatures

orbit—the path an object follows as it goes around the sun or a planet

oxygen—a colorless gas that people breathe; humans and animals need oxygen to live

rotation—the motion of an object around an internal axis

satellite—an object in space that circles a larger object, such as a planet

sulfur—a yellow chemical element that burns easily and is very smelly

Deep Thoughts with Mr. Kazarian

This story combines fiction (made-up) and nonfiction (true) elements. What are two true things you learned about planets from this story?

- Each of the four kids in the story has his or her own interests and hobbies. Can you name one fact each about TJ, Shea, Walden, and Dani?

- Mr. Kazarian works as a librarian on Earth. What qualities do you think a great librarian should have?

- Mrs. Tsao, the science teacher, assigns a research project on gas giants. What kind of project would you make to show what you learned about gas giants?

- Mr. Kazarian comes from a fictional alien planet. If you created a made-up planet, what would it look like and what kind of aliens would live there?

Read More

Baker, Theo. *Gas Giant Jump*. Galaxy Games. Vero Beach, FL: Rourke Educational Media, 2017.

Cruddas, Sarah. *Solar System*. DKfindout! New York: DK Publishing, 2016.

Radomski, Kassandra. *The Secrets of Saturn*. Planets. North Mankato, MN: Capstone Press, 2015.

Spilsbury, Richard. *Space.* Adventures in STEAM. North Mankato, MN: Capstone Press, 2018.

Steve →

Steve Foxe is the author of more than 20 children's books and comics for properties including Pokémon, Transformers, Adventure Time, Steven Universe, DC Super Friends, and Grumpy Cat. He is the editor of *Paste* magazine's comic section and lives in Queens, New York, where he thinks a lot about cats, even ones who can't shoot lasers from their eyes.

Gary →

Gary Boller is an illustrator and animator based in London. He has written and illustrated many children's books and comics, including strips for *The Beano, The Dandy,* and *The Times.* He also works in advertising and entertainment, including the Bafta winning animated series, The Amazing Adrenalini Brothers. Gary, too, is never very far away from a cat and is unwittingly helping them take control of this planet.

Mr. Kazarian, Alien Librarian is published by Stone Arch Books,
a Capstone Imprint
1710 Roe Crest Drive
North Mankato, Minnesota 56003
www.capstonepub.com

Library of Congress Cataloging-in-Publication Data
Names: Foxe, Steve, author. | Boller, Gary, illustrator.
Title: Mr. Kazarian, alien librarian / by Steve Foxe ; illustrated by Gary Boller.
Description: North Mankato, Minnesota : Stone Arch Books, a Capstone Imprint,
   [2020] | Series: Mr. Kazarian, alien librarian ; 1 | Summary: Mr.
   Kazarian, the school librarian, is actually an extraterrestrial (with a
   holographic disguise) studying the behavior of human children, and if he
   wants to continue his research he will have to find a way to convince the
   four students who have discovered his secret not to expose him—perhaps by
   helping their assignment on gas giants with a quick trip to space.
Identifiers: LCCN 2018054841 (print) | LCCN 2018057513 (ebook) | ISBN
   9781496583710 (ebook PDF) | ISBN 9781496583666 (hardcover)
Subjects: LCSH: Extraterrestrial beings—Comic books, strips, etc. |
   Extraterrestrial beings—Juvenile fiction. | Librarians—Comic books,
   strips, etc. | Librarians—Juvenile fiction. | School field trips—Comic
   books, strips, etc. | School field trips—Juvenile fiction. | Graphic
   novels. | Jupiter (Planet)—Comic books, strips, etc. | Jupiter
   (Planet)—Juvenile fiction. | CYAC: Graphic novels. | Extraterrestrial
   Beings—Fiction. | Librarians—Fiction. | School field trips—Fiction. |
   Jupiter (Planet)—Fiction. | LCGFT: Graphic novels.
Classification: LCC PZ7.1.F694 (ebook) | LCC PZ7.7.F69 Mr 2020 (print) |
   DDC 741.5/973—dc23
LC record available at https://lccn.loc.gov/2018054841

Editorial Credits
Kristen Mohn, editor; Ted Williams, designer; Kelly Garvin, media researcher;
Tori Abraham, production specialist

Printed in the United States of America.
PA71